LUCY'S DETECTIVE FORM

PREESHA

Copyright © Preesha
All Rights Reserved.

This book has been published with all efforts taken to make the material error-free after the consent of the author. However, the author and the publisher do not assume and hereby disclaim any liability to any party for any loss, damage, or disruption caused by errors or omissions, whether such errors or omissions result from negligence, accident, or any other cause.

While every effort has been made to avoid any mistake or omission, this publication is being sold on the condition and understanding that neither the author nor the publishers or printers would be liable in any manner to any person by reason of any mistake or omission in this publication or for any action taken or omitted to be taken or advice rendered or accepted on the basis of this work. For any defect in printing or binding the publishers will be liable only to replace the defective copy by another copy of this work then available.

"Mrs. Morean! Mrs Morean!" Lucy shouted as she ran to the house. She found

Mrs. Morean waiting to see her, with a surprised look on her face. "Mrs. Morean, I just found a clue!" " What's the clue? Tell me!"

"Okay, look here! A ring! And I know I saw it here!"

Madame Gay Lady, (was what Mrs Morean liked to call herself), picked up the ring and took it for closer inspection. "That's not a clue! That's my cousin Katy's ring, I do believe!"

"mmm... who's Katy?"

"Katy's come to stay. She would be delighted if you gave her ring."

"Oh yeah, Katy. But look, here's a cat's face. Your cousin must love cats. I saw one here."

"Yup. On the ring the cat's face that is carved is Katy's cat. Katy sure does love cats. Sometimes we expand her name to Cat Lady. Come I'll show Katy to you." she concluded, jogging a little as she ascended to her cousin's room, Lucy following.

Gay Lady opened the door and Lucy peeped in timidly. A thin, miserly-looking lady with four adorable kittens in her lap looked up at her with an angry look at Lucy, as if she had disturbed Katy thoroughly. She had light brown eyes, a stubby nose, and paleness throughout her face. Lucy didn't quite like the look of her. But she thought Mrs. Morean might feel bad if she left too soon. So, admiring the cute kittens from afar, longing to stroke their soft like velvet fur, she spent a few more minutes, gazing up in wonder every ten seconds. Then she left, her gown touching the frequently cleaned marble ground. She told her host, "I enjoyed the company of your cousin and her cats." Actually, she didn't like Mrs. Morean's cousin at all, but, as I already told you, she admired the cats.

Shockingly, that day as Lucy was about to leave, she heard a loud voice saying, "Hey you! What do you think you're doing? First wash the dishes, iron the clothes and lay out my cats' and their kittens' food, and then eat yours!" Lucy could guess it was Katy, but when she looked over her shoulder, Katy was saying that to Martha. Lucy could not imagine that someone could be so rude to a person so good-natured as Martha. She said to herself, "Maybe there was a minor quarrel between the two of them."

Next morning she woke up and, remembering it was Monday, met her disappointment.

Still, after school she assembled all the clues, Martha's eye evidence, and the cat head ring. One morning she woke up to find it was Saturday! Lucy had lost track of the days, and all she seemed to do was wait all week.

Chp3-Martha's Arrest

Off she set, acting like an official detective, creeping as quietly as a mouse. She reached Mrs Morean's house to hear a loud sobbing from the inside. She put her ear to the closed door and listened. "Noo! I don't want this to happen!" This statement made Lucy curious and she peeked through an open window. She saw a policeman in a smart black uniform, saying he had to take Martha. The girls, Ana and Loi-Loi, were the ones sobbing. Lucy privately thought she shouldn't enter the house openly in such a situation. Still, she couldn't resist the temptation to peek in again and see what would happen next. Madame Gay Lady called Martha and she came immediately, and when she saw the policeman she did not panic at all, instead she smiled. That big, warm, nice smile that she had smiled when she first saw Lucy.

"Please take a seat." Lucy looked around. So did the policeman. There were sofas with the most luxurious soft pillows. The sofa covers were in all the colours of the rainbow. "We sit when we have come from a long journey, for a long time. But I have come to take Martha Shamble to our police station, and I will leave now." The policeman added, addressing Martha, "Come quietly or you will be taken in force." Lucy was peeping in from the front window near the door. She quickly darted toward the side and lay flat. Martha and the policeman passed by her. She let out a sigh of relief. Now that this wonderful lady was arrested, she was determined to solve the mystery more than ever!

Chp4-The Mystery is Solved

Now Lucy sat racking her brains and pondering over what she already knew at the dinner table. She wondered if anyone had gone unnoticed and decided tomorrow to get all the names of the home guards. She went and asked Nick of the people's names. Although he gave her a stern and suspicious look, he told Lucy all the details. "Your name's Lucy right?" he started, but when Lucy nodded gravely, he thought he might get onto the subject. "Okay, so there's Martha as you know, whom everyone likes, and then there's Goel, who couldn't have done it, because he retires for the night and goes to his house, which is miles away. And then there's a drunken guard, Sim, who was tied up so he couldn't have done it either...."

"Hey! All you're telling me is who couldn't have done it! Tell me who *could* have done it! Could, could, could!" "Patience! Now I'm frustrated too! I won't tell you anything now!" screamed back Nick. "Well, I don't care anymore! I'll do this! Don't need your help, Nick!" Lucy said. She was confident that she would solve the mystery, but she felt a little bad that she had screamed at Nick who was older than her. She tried to forget it. Her tries went all in vain. So she decided to apologize the next day. She remembered the cat head ring and looked for more clues. She found something circular and curved like a hemisphere. She took it home and asked her mother what it was. Her mother said it was a contact lens. The next day was Tuesday and Lucy looked up contact lenses in her ICT class. She found the perfect solution to how the robbery could have been done. She analysed and remembered an unknown suspect...

Next evening, (she couldn't bear to wait till Saturday) she set out for Tipputie for the last time. She was sad she wouldn't see it again. But she hurried to reach there. And when she did, she explained how the robbery would have been done. "Mrs. Morean, Nick, Ana, Loi-Loi, Katy, and everybody else, I have news to tell!" Everybody heard her shouts and gathered around her. "What news, Lucy?" Gay Lady said. "The mystery is solved! I told you, Nick!" Nick was speechless and his mouth fell open. "What? How? Who?" everyone chanted. "Come on now, let's all sit down comfortably and talk, it's a long story.

"Look at this, it's the same cat head ring that I showed you before, belonging to Katy. Katy loves cats, doesn't she? Well Katy, take it back. And here, what is this?"

"What is this? What is this?" repeated the Morean and Sim and Goel.

"It's a contact lens. Did you know there also came contact lenses?"

Everybody was silent.

"And someone wearing colour contact lenses imitated Martha with her sea blue eyes. Do you know who that is?"

"Whoever it is, he or she should be punished! Yes!!!!"

"You all will be fair surprised. It's your very own.....Katy!"

"And what evidence do you have?" said Katy angrily.

"I don't have evidence, but I know you have a motive!"

"And what is that?"

"I don't know. Few days back, you were shouting at Martha for some reason!"

Now Mrs Morean rose from her chair and, looking at Lucy, she said, "You are right. I overheard a conversation nights before the theft, Katy saying Martha had humiliated her in some way, and Martha was just trying to reason with her when she got as angry as an erupting volcano. Then I guess she robbed the house on Martha's behalf as revenge."

Katy started her drama now. She fell down to the ground crying like a baby. "Please forgive me. I did all this only because of the nearby kids who called me boring. I've buried all that I have stolen in the garden of this very house. I didn't really mean any harm. It's only because of my uncontrolled anger that I got Martha into all this." she concluded, now a little puddle of tears forming around her.

"We'll see what to do with you later. Now let's get Martha out of jail."
Lucy said wisely.

Later, when Martha came back and Katy went in her place, Lucy
taunted Nick a little, and then made friends with him and his sisters.
Martha was made chief servant. As for Katy, she lived in jail for the
rest of her life, always trying to find ways to evade prison.
Occasionally, she got a little tip from her cousin and Katy's nephew
and nieces, who sometimes felt sorry for her. Poor Katy! Though she
did get what she deserved!

And we will leave the Morean family, Martha and her assistants, and
of course dear Lucy just there. Till Lucy's next adventure!

Contents

CHAPTER ONE

The Robber

Chp1-The Robbery

Lucy was pretty surprised when her father read out the headlines of the newspaper to her." Another robbery in town. At The Morean Family Home." Lucy urged her father to resume reading. "The police are clueless and the Morean family is on the verge of tears." This silenced Lucy and her mother.

Lucy was a gentle, beautiful girl. But she was not only that. She was also an unrecognized detective, deep down. This was her chance to do something big. She was ecstatic when she heard the news. The weekend came, and Lucy set off to investigate!

The wind was breezy, and the sun was at its maximum temperature. Wearing a thin, pretty blue-and-yellow frock, Lucy went up the hill at the Morean family's home. She had got the address in the newspaper. The Cottage name was Tipputie, no. 22 from the edge of the street.

Lucy knocked at the door. She was quickly taken in. She decided that she would befriend the Morean children, and she found it was easier than she had thought, because they liked her very much. The one older than her, his name was Nick, and the two girls younger than Lucy, their names were Ana and Loi-Loi. She asked Mrs Morean about the theft. Mrs Morean didn't mind telling her. "Ah, a detective in the form of little Lucy! Well, I'll tell you. Indeed, it was a very clever theft. If the robber was an outsider, it is surprising that the home guards don't know who it was. And if you're asking if the thief was among them, the others would have surely told me .My husband, Solir, was awake and watching. My husband had woken up from a dream that said our house would get robbed. And it was true!"

"Who is the main suspect?" asked Lucy, growing curious now.

"Our faithful maid Martha. She is such a sweet old dear, that I cannot believe it was her. Though, the evidence was that Solir was watching, as I already told you, saw the unmistakable flashing blue eyes of Martha, creeping out of the house. He even took a photograph."

"mmm...Interesting case...mmm." murmured the now deep in thought Lucy. "Can I meet this Martha?"

"Certainly. We don't have full proof, so Martha isn't arrested yet. This way." Mrs Morean led Lucy to the kitchen. A plump old lady was scrubbing utensils vigorously. She had a hooked nose and enchanting blue eyes. She stared at Lucy, and then she smiled.

Lucy couldn't believe this wonderful lady could have been the thief. Even more wonderful was the fact that she could smile when she was in such a position that could have been worse than torture.

So Lucy looked for other suspects, and clues. She went around the house, garden, and greenhouse. She found a gold ring behind a bush. It looked suspiciously like somebody had purposely left it there, such a good hiding place it was. It had a cat's head carved on it. Lucy felt she had seen it before that day. However, she could not memorize where she had seen it, how much ever she tried.

She went to bed with that unsatisfied feeling in her stomach.

CHAPTER TWO

A Clue Understood

A Clue Understood

Next morning, she woke up very, very happy. She had had a dream that she solved the puzzling mystery. And she also remembered where she had seen the cat's face. She stuffed herself with her breakfast and ran back to Cottage no.22, very energetic.

"Mrs. Morean! Mrs Morean!" Lucy shouted as she ran to the house. She found

Mrs. Morean waiting to see her, with a surprised look on her face. "Mrs. Morean, I just found a clue!" " What's the clue? Tell me!"

"Okay, look here! A ring! And I know I saw it here!"

Madame Gay Lady, (was what Mrs Morean liked to call herself), picked up the ring and took it for closer inspection. "That's not a clue! That's my cousin Katy's ring, I do believe!"

"mmm... who's Katy?"

"Katy's come to stay. She would be delighted if you gave her ring."

"Oh yeah, Katy. But look, here's a cat's face. Your cousin must love cats. I saw one here."

"Yup. On the ring the cat's face that is carved is Katy's cat. Katy sure does love cats. Sometimes we expand her name to Cat Lady. Come I'll show Katy to you." she concluded, jogging a little as she ascended to her cousin's room, Lucy following.

Gay Lady opened the door and Lucy peeped in timidly. A thin, miserly-looking lady with four adorable kittens in her lap looked up at her with an angry look at Lucy, as if she had disturbed Katy thoroughly. She had light brown eyes, a stubby nose, and paleness throughout her face. Lucy didn't quite like the look of her. But she thought Mrs. Morean might feel bad if she left too soon. So, admiring the cute kittens from afar, longing to stroke their soft like velvet fur, she spent a few more minutes, gazing up in wonder every ten seconds. Then she left, her gown touching the frequently cleaned marble ground. She told her host, "I enjoyed the company of your cousin and her cats." Actually, she didn't like Mrs. Morean's cousin at all, but, as I already told you, she admired the cats.

Shockingly, that day as Lucy was about to leave, she heard a loud voice saying, "Hey you! What do you think you're doing? First wash the dishes, iron the clothes and lay out my cats' and their kittens' food, and then eat yours!" Lucy could guess it was Katy, but when she looked over her shoulder, Katy was saying that to Martha. Lucy could not imagine that someone could be so rude to a person so good-natured as Martha. She said to herself, "Maybe there was a minor quarrel between the two of them."

Next morning she woke up and, remembering it was Monday, met her disappointment.

Still, after school she assembled all the clues, Martha's eye evidence, and the cat head ring. One morning she woke up to find it was Saturday! Lucy had lost track of the days, and all she seemed to do was wait all week.

CHAPTER THREE

Martha's Arrest

-Martha's Arrest

Off she set, acting like an official detective, creeping as quietly as a mouse. She reached Mrs Morean's house to hear a loud sobbing from the inside. She put her ear to the closed door and listened. "Noo! I don't want this to happen!" This statement made Lucy curious and she peeked through an open window. She saw a policeman in a smart black uniform, saying he had to take Martha. The girls, Ana and Loi- Loi, were the ones sobbing. Lucy privately thought she shouldn't enter the house openly in such a situation. Still, she couldn't resist the temptation to peek in again and see what would happen next. Madame Gay Lady called Martha and she came immediately, and when she saw the policeman she did not panic at all, instead she smiled. That big, warm, nice smile that she had smiled when she first saw Lucy.

"Please take a seat." Lucy looked around. So did the policeman. There were sofas with the most luxurious soft pillows. The sofa covers were in all the colours of the rainbow. "We sit when we have come from a long journey, for a long time. But I have come to take Martha Shamble to our police station, and I will leave now." The policeman added, addressing Martha, "Come quietly or you will be taken in force." Lucy was peeping in from the front window near the door. She quickly darted toward the side and lay flat. Martha and the policeman passed by her. She let out a sigh of relief. Now that this wonderful lady was arrested, she was determined to solve the mystery more than ever!

CHAPTER FOUR

The Mystery is Solved

Now Lucy sat racking her brains and pondering over what she already knew at the dinner table. She wondered if anyone had gone unnoticed and decided tomorrow to get all the names of the home guards. She went and asked Nick of the people's names. Although he gave her a stern and suspicious look, he told Lucy all the details. "Your name's Lucy right?" he started, but when Lucy nodded gravely, he thought he might get onto the subject. "Okay, so there's Martha as you know, whom everyone likes, and then there's Goel, who couldn't have done it, because he retires for the night and goes to his house, which is miles away. And then there's a drunken guard, Sim, who was tied up so he couldn't have done it either...."

"Hey! All you're telling me is who couldn't have done it! Tell me who *could* have done it! Could, could, could!" "Patience! Now I'm frustrated too! I won't tell you anything now!" screamed back Nick. "Well, I don't care anymore! I'll do this! Don't need your help, Nick!" Lucy said. She was confident that she would solve the mystery, but she felt a little bad that she had screamed at Nick who was older than her. She tried to forget it. Her tries went all in vain. So she decided to apologize the next day. She remembered the cat head ring and looked for more clues. She found something circular and curved like a hemisphere. She took it home and asked her mother what it was. Her mother said it was a contact lens. The next day was Tuesday and Lucy looked up contact lenses in her ICT class. She found the perfect solution to how the robbery could have been done. She analysed and remembered an unknown suspect...

Next evening, (she couldn't bear to wait till Saturday) she set out for Tipputie for the last time. She was sad she wouldn't see it again. But she hurried to reach there. And when she did, she explained how the robbery would have been done. "Mrs. Morean